Elizabeth Gordon

An imprint of Enslow Publishing

WEST **44** BOOKS™

Milo on Wheels

Javi Takes a Bow

Addy's Big Splash

Noah the Con Artist

Club Zoe

Please visit our website, www.west44books.com. For a free color catalog of all our high-quality books, call toll free 1-800-542-2595 or fax 1-877-542-2596.

Cataloging-in-Publication Data

Names: Gordon, Elizabeth.
Title: Addy's big splash / Elizabeth Gordon.
Description: New York : West 44, 2020. | Series: The club
Identifiers: ISBN 9781538382431 (pbk.) | ISBN 9781538382448 (library bound) | ISBN 9781538383223 (ebook)
Subjects: LCSH: Friendship--Juvenile fiction. | After-school programs--Juvenile fiction. | Swimming--Juvenile fiction. | Teamwork (Sports)--Juvenile fiction. | Competition (Psychology)--Juvenile fiction.
Classification: LCC PZ7.G673 Ad 2020 | DDC [F]--dc23

First Edition

Published in 2020 by
Enslow Publishing
111 East 14th Street, Suite 349
New York, NY 10003

Copyright © 2020 Enslow Publishing

Editor: Theresa Emminizer
Designer: Sam DeMartin
Interior Layout: Rachel Rising

Photo Credits: Photo Credits: front matter (basketball) LHF Graphics/Shutterstock.com; front matter (planets) Nikolaeva/Shutterstock.com; pp. 1, 7 16, 32, 40, 47, 54, 61 (hurricane) GO BANANAS DESIGN STUDIO/Shutterstock.com; front matter (stickers) U.Pimages_vector/Shutterstock.com; front matter (paint splatter) Milan M/Shutterstock.com; front matter (boomerang) hchjjl/Shutterstock.com; front matter (game strategy) Dejan Popovic/Shutterstock.com; front matter (broken bone) BlueRingMedia/Shutterstock.com; front matter (Guatemala stamp) astudio/Shutterstock.com; front matter (bandaids) lineartestpilot/Shutterstock.com; front matter (ants) Viktorija Reuta/Shutterstock.com; front matter (billboard) Franzi/Shutterstock.com; p. 1 jane55/Shutterstock.com; pp. 2, 16 LHF Graphics/Shutterstock.com; p. 4 Tatahnka/Shutterstock.com; p. 5, 20 wong salam/Shutterstock.com; p. 7 Kamieshkova/Shutterstock.com; p. 9 AuraArt/Shutterstock.com; p. 10 agentgirl05/Shutterstock.com; p. 12 NikomMaelao Production/Shutterstock.com; p. 18 Dewberry_Riya/Shutterstock.com; pp. 22, 23 BatikArt/Shutterstock.com; p. 24 olllikeballoon/Shutterstock.com; pp. 26, 42 serg_65/Shutterstock.com; pp. 27, 55, 56 Lemonade Serenade/Shutterstock.com; pp. 30, 51, 65, 66 Emmeewhite/Shutterstock.com; p. 36 wenchiawang/Shutterstock.com; p. 37 doodleboards/Shutterstock.com; p. 46 Huza/Shutterstock.com; p. 50 josep perianes jorba/Shutterstock.com; p. 52 Prokhorovich/Shutterstock.com; p. 59 hudhud94/Shutterstock.com; p. hchjjl/Shutterstock.com; p. 62 olllikeballoon/Shutterstock.com; p. 66 dicogm/Shutterstock.com; p. 68 mhatzapa/Shutterstock.com; p. 72 Milan M/Shutterstock.com.

Printed in the United States of America

CPSIA compliance information: Batch #CS18W44: For further information contact
Enslow Publishing, New York, New York at 1-800-542-2595.

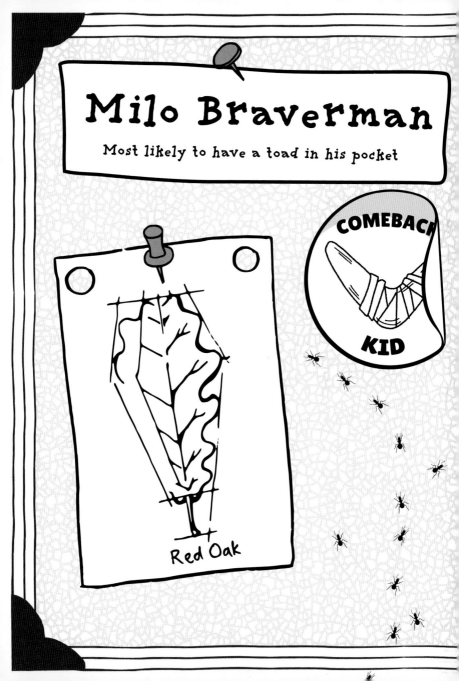

GUATEMALA ★ GUATEMALA ★ REPÚBLICA DE GUATEMALA

Guatemala

EMBODIMENT OF TEVYE

Javi Morales

Most likely to know all the words to *Hamilton*

Chapter One
Hurricane Addy

Addy's Monday began with a smash.

It happened in first period Biology. Addy was late. She hurried to her lab table. She swung her backpack onto the desk. The backpack knocked against a cart. A rolling cart full of glass jars.

Crash! Crash! Crash! Three jars tipped off the cart. They smashed on the floor. Pale, flabby lab specimens slid across the tile. A strong, sharp

smell filled the air. Her classmates screamed. "Clear the room!" shouted her teacher. Gagging, Addy said, "I'm so sorry, Ms. Park! Can I help you clean…"

"No," said Ms. Park firmly. She threw open all the windows. "Thank you, Addy. But *please* don't help."

The kids gathered in the hallway. A boy laughed. "Hurricane Addy strikes again!"

Hurricane Addy.

Again.

The name had followed Addy for a long time. Ever since she'd tried out for the school's field

hockey team. In just ten minutes, she'd sent not one but two teammates to the nurse's office. The coach took her stick away. He suggested that she might like volleyball.

Addy thought that could be a good idea. She had grown three inches over the summer. She towered over her classmates. Volleyball was supposed to be a good sport for tall kids.

The volleyball coach was excited about her height. She put Addy in the center of the front row. "You'll make a great middle blocker," she said.

Addy lasted a little longer at this tryout. But other players kept missing the ball. They were too busy avoiding Addy's long arms and legs.

"Addy!" the coach called. "Stop spinning around like a hurricane!"

Addy tried. But she wasn't sure where her legs and arms were. They'd grown so quickly. Sometimes, they seemed like they belonged to

someone else.

The more embarrassed Addy felt, the more clumsy she got. As she stumbled off the court, she heard the coach say, "She looks like a baby giraffe on ice."

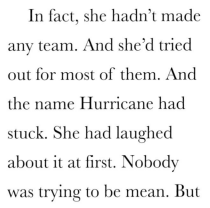

She didn't make the team.

In fact, she hadn't made any team. And she'd tried out for most of them. And the name Hurricane had stuck. She had laughed about it at first. Nobody was trying to be mean. But she hadn't thought the nickname would last. It was starting to annoy her.

After all, she wasn't the only kid that had broken a bone. OK, *bones*. And, yes, accidents did seem to happen around her. A lot. But anybody

could saw a picnic table in half by mistake. Or knock over a bunch of jars in the science lab. Or know their emergency room doctors by name. There was no reason to make such a big deal about it.

There was also no reason for the cafeteria janitor to grab for his mop when Addy picked up her tray. Or for her art teacher, Hannah, to say, "Why don't I get that for you?" when Addy reached for some pottery. Or for her violin teacher, Mr. Almadani, to sit far away when she played. "I can hear you better from here," he'd said.

OK, she kind of understood that one. She *had* poked him a few times with her bow. But still.

She didn't want to be known for being a klutz. She was actually *good* at lots of things. She could be Honor Roll Addy or Tutoring Addy. Musical Addy or Organizing Addy. Great at Talking Addy or Awesome with Kids Addy. But no. People didn't pay attention to any of that. They just joked about how clumsy she was.

Addy worried that she was going to be known as Hurricane Addy forever. She could think of only one way to shake the nickname. She needed to succeed at a sport. That's what people cared about.

But try as she might, Addy couldn't figure out how to do that.

Chapter Two
Ana

Addy walked through the January snow into Parkside Community Center. She was still thinking about the lab accident. She was glad no one else at her after-school program, The Club, was in Ms. Park's class. Only a few kids  even went to her school. She didn't need another Addy disaster story going around.

"Hey, Addy!" Her friend Zoe crossed the front hall to meet her. "Heard you cleared your biology room this morning. Way to get out of class!"

"How do you know about that?" Addy said. She was shocked. Zoe didn't even go to her school.

"Noah told me," Zoe answered.

Zoe's twin brother? "But how does *he* know?" Addy asked.

"He has a buddy at your school. Word got around. Did they really have to call the fire department?"

"What? No! Is that what he said?"

Zoe shrugged. "You know how rumors are." She grinned. "Wait until tomorrow. People will be saying you set the whole school on fire."

Addy groaned. They walked into The Club's snack area. Their friend Milo was sitting at a table. It looked like he was studying something. He

looked up when Addy slumped into a chair beside him.

"Hey, Addy!" said Milo. "Did you really—"

"No!" said Addy. She dropped her head in her hands. "I don't want to talk about it, Milo."

Milo laughed. "That's a first. You usually like to talk about everything. All the time."

Zoe frowned at Milo. "Don't be embarrassed, Addy," she said. "You got your whole class out of biology. Everyone thinks that's awesome!" She shook her long braids. "I wish you went to my school. Maybe you could get me out of math."

Addy rolled her eyes at Zoe. She just didn't understand. How could she?

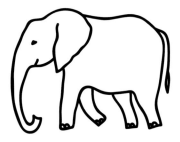

Addy often felt like a lumbering, redheaded elephant around Zoe. She was pretty and popular.

She was good at sports. She was captain of The Club's basketball team. She got asked to dances.

In other words, Zoe was…successful. Nobody gave her embarrassing nicknames. Or thought she was a klutz. Everybody took her seriously.

Addy shook herself. She wanted to change the subject. She pointed at Milo's book, one about nature. Milo loved nature. "What are you working on so hard?"

Milo's face lit up. He showed her a few pine cones. "I'm trying to figure out what kind of tree these belong to."

Addy smiled. Milo would have liked seeing the lab specimens. He might have even known what they were.

He wanted to be a biologist when he grew up. He

was always drawing or writing in his field guide. It was filled with pictures and information about plants and animals. Milo loved finding new things to add to it.

Zoe picked up the pine cones. "Did Javi give you these?" she asked. Their friend Javi often found things in the park. He'd bring them to Milo.

"No," Milo said. "There was no snow yesterday. The ground was nice and hard. I could get out on my crutches." Addy nodded. Milo's legs were in braces. He had to use crutches to walk. Bad weather made it hard for him to go exploring.

"Where is Javi, anyway?" asked Zoe, looking around. Javi usually joined them for something to eat at the beginning of Club. Then he and Addy would start their tutoring session. Addy was helping Javi with English and schoolwork. His family had moved to town last summer from Guatemala.

Just then, Javi walked into the snack area. Miguel, the big, tattooed club director, was with him. So was a little girl. She had the same straight, dark hair as Javi. She was holding his hand. She looked shyly around her with big, brown eyes.

"Ana!" Addy said. She got up and hugged the girl. "You came!" Ana gave her a nervous smile. Addy had met Javi's seven-year-old sister once before. She had come to see Javi in the winter musical last month. Addy had shown her around the stage set. Ana didn't speak much English. But they had hit it off anyway.

Addy knew how much Javi wanted Ana to come to The Club. He thought it would be good

for her. He had spent months trying to get her to come. But Ana was very shy in her new country. She had been scared to ride the bus or meet so many strangers. This was a big step for her.

Miguel smiled. "Ana is just visiting today. Tomorrow, she'll come full-time."

"Wow!" said Addy. "Are you going to do some activities, Ana?"

Javi repeated the question to her in Spanish. Ana nodded and spoke to Javi. "She say," said Javi in his thick accent, "she is liking art and music. And we both swimming."

"Great!" Addy said. She looked at Ana. "Are you excited?"

"Yes," said Javi, before Ana could answer. "We have no swimming where we come from. It is very exciting."

Ana pulled on Javi's hand and spoke to him in Spanish. Miguel laughed.

"I think you have a fan, Addy," said Miguel. "Ana wants to know if you are going to take swim lessons, too."

Addy smiled at Ana and shook her head. "No, I already know how to swim," she said. She took Ana's hand. "But I will see you around, okay?"

Ana smiled, too. She and Javi turned to follow Miguel. Ana looked back over her shoulder.

Addy waved. "*Hasta mañana*," she called.

Ana grinned. "*Hasta mañana…* Add-dee," she said.

Addy turned back around. Noah had joined them at the table. "Hey, Hurricane!" he said excitedly. "Tell us how you shut down your whole school!"

"Noah," she said. "My name is Addy."

She sighed. It had been nice, for a moment, to talk with someone who didn't know her by any

other name.

Chapter Three
Ins and Outs

Addy picked at her dinner of warmed-up Chinese leftovers. Her mom sat across from her. She was studying a textbook while she ate.

Finally, her mom broke the silence. "You're very quiet tonight, Addy. You're usually full of stories."

"I…I caused a little accident at school today,

Mom," Addy said. "You might get a call."

Her mom didn't even look up. She was used to this sort of news. "Are we talking about the lab jars or something else?"

Surprised, Addy said, "The lab jars."

"Oh, yeah," her mom said. "I already talked to Ms. Park about that. She wasn't too upset. You are her star student, after all. I said we'd replace them." She pointed at a paragraph in her book. "But I did make one suggestion. She should avoid putting rolling carts near your desk. There should be proper regulations. That could be neglect!"

Addy's mom was putting herself through law school. She was always trying out legal terms. Addy shrugged and shook her head.

"Either way," she said. "I'm still the idiot."

"Addison," her mom said. "You are NOT an idiot. You're one of the smartest people I know. You can, however, be a little careless. You charge

into things without thinking. And right now, your body is going through an awkward phase."

"Very awkward," Addy said.

"Okay, very awkward," said her mom, laughing. "But you won't always feel like a fish out of water. You'll grow out of it."

"I don't think I need to do any more growing, Mom," Addy said. "I'm already the tallest kid in my class."

"Don't be ashamed of your height, honey. You're the perfect size for you. Learn to be comfortable in your own skin."

Addy fell silent. She nibbled at a cold egg roll. Her mom had been a star soccer player in high school. She was small and quick. Addy was pretty sure she'd never had an awkward day in her life.

Addy got her height from her dad. At least, that's what her mom said. Addy had to take her word for it. She'd never met him. It wasn't fair. She'd gotten all her worst features from her father. But she couldn't make him feel bad about it.

The next day, Addy was in The Club's music room. She was finishing her violin lesson. Mr. Almadani said, "Excellent, Addy! You worked hard on that piece." Javi walked in. Ana was with him.

"Javi!" said Mr. Almadani, smiling. "Good to see you!"

Javi grinned. Mr. Almadani and Javi had become good friends during the musical.

"And who is this?" Mr. Almadani asked. He peered over his glasses at Ana. She was staring at all the instruments. She looked stunned. Like she'd walked through a strange door. Then found herself in a wonderland.

Javi introduced his sister. Mr. Almadani

asked if she wanted a tour. Javi translated the question. Ana nodded excitedly. She had lost all her shyness.

Javi watched Ana for a minute, smiling. Then he turned to Addy. "You help me? My sister swims today. She not know how…" He paused, trying to think of the right words. "How to be dressing?"

"Oh," said Addy. "She doesn't know how to use the girls' locker room?"

Javi nodded. "You help?"

"Sure," said Addy. "I'll take her through."

They turned at the sound of music. Ana was holding a guitar in her lap. She was playing a simple little song. "Javi," said Mr. Almadani. He sounded

surprised and pleased. "You didn't tell me your sister could play guitar."

Javi nodded. "*Un poco*," he said. "A little. My father teach us. In Guatemala." He checked the clock. "We go now, Ana. Time for swim class."

Ana handed Mr. Almadani the guitar. "You must come back, young lady," the music teacher said. "You clearly belong here. Like Addy."

Ana smiled. Addy thought she'd come back every chance she got.

Chapter Four
The Swim Team

Addy took Ana into the changing room. She showed her how to use the lockers. She pointed out the curtained stalls. Ana went in one and put on her suit. She talked to Addy the whole time in Spanish. She sounded excited and happy. Addy had picked up a little Spanish from

Javi. But she couldn't really understand. So she just nodded. She thought Ana might still be talking about the music room.

Then Addy took Ana's hand. She led her out to swim class. Miguel was standing at one end of the pool. He was in his swimsuit. Javi and a few younger kids were gathered around him.

Ana stopped. Addy felt her stiffen. The relaxed, happy look on her face went away. She stopped and stared around her. The pool was huge. The Club's swim team was working at the far end. Their noisy shouts and whistles echoed all over the big room.

Addy thought Ana was trying to understand what she was getting into. Probably she had never seen a pool like this. Javi said they had never done any swimming. Addy wondered if Ana had ever

been in any water other than a tub.

Addy tried to lead Ana forward. The little girl clung to her hand and held back. "It's OK," Addy said. "Swimming is fun!"

Javi came up and spoke to her in Spanish. Ana shook her head. She seemed close to tears.

Addy had an idea. She pulled off her shoes and rolled up her jeans. "Come on, Ana," she said. "Let's sit and watch." She walked over to the

side of the pool. She sat down and patted a place beside her. Ana looked unsure. She sat down. But she kept far away from the edge of the pool.

"Way to go, Addy," Miguel said quietly. "I'm going to start working with the others. See if you can get her to put her feet in."

Addy and Ana watched the swim class begin. Javi and the other kids followed Miguel's directions. Javi was pretty fearless. He put his face in right away.

Addy got Ana to dip her toes in the pool. Then she dripped water on Ana's legs and made her giggle. Miguel came back over. He tried to get Ana to join him in the water. But Ana would not go in.

"Please keep sitting with her, Addy," Miguel said. "She's going to need some time."

So Addy sat with Ana. They watched the class. And Addy pointed out the swim team. They

were winding up their practice with races. "Just think, Ana. You could swim like that some day," she said.

The team was certainly fun to watch. The swimmers sped through the water like dolphins. Addy knew they won competitions all the time. They had a shelf full of trophies in the front hall.

She remembered what her mom had said. *You won't always feel like a fish out of water.* Well, she thought, maybe that was her problem. Maybe she needed to get *in* the water. After all, long arms and legs were good for swimming. And how could she hurt herself or anyone else in a pool?

Addy imagined herself on a championship swim team. Why not? She could already swim well.

She'd spent every summer with her grandparents. They had a house by the lake. She'd been in the water since she was a baby. And she always beat her cousins at races to the raft.

She pictured people cheering as she cut smoothly through the water. Watching her win swim meets. Seeing her name on a swim trophy in the front hall. They couldn't call her Hurricane then. She'd finally lose her nickname. She'd get some respect.

Addy looked at Javi's sister. "Ana," she said, "You and I are going to *own* this pool. I promise."

Ana glanced up at her and smiled. She didn't really understand. So she just nodded.

Ana's class ended. Addy steered her back to the locker room. Then she walked over to the swim coach's office. Practice had been over for a while. But swimmers still chatted in little groups as they dried off.

Addy had gone to The Club since she was in preschool. She recognized many of the kids on the team. But she didn't know them well. Swimmers were known to be a little intense. They practiced all the time. And they often hung out near their coach's office after they were done.

Coach Meg had short, shocking pink hair and a nose ring. She wore a sweatshirt that said "Just Keep Swimming." Addy asked her about joining. Coach Meg said, "Sure you can!" She handed Addy a form to fill out. "There are no tryouts. Everyone practices together. You can come two to five times a week. It depends on how much you want to do. But I need to test you. Come near

the end of practice tomorrow. We'll see how fast you are. Then we can get you in the right practice group."

"When are the swim meets?" asked Addy. She was eager to start competing.

The coach pulled a schedule off her clipboard. "Not everyone on the team races. You'll go to a swim meet when you're ready. There's one coming up in about four weeks."

Addy turned to go. She was excited. She walked past a few swimmers sitting on the bleachers. One of them turned and glanced at her. A girl with freckles. Addy recognized her from school. Wasn't her name Erin? Someone in her grade but not in her classes.

Addy didn't think much about it. She reached the locker room door. Just then, she heard the echo of a whisper. "Hurricane Addy is joining the swim team? Let me tell you what she did

yesterday…"

Addy turned her head. The little group of swimmers was giggling.

Addy pushed open the door. Sometimes it was better not to hear.

"The swim team?" her mom said that night. "You want to join the swim team? Do you have time? What about violin, and tutoring, and schoolwork?"

"I can make it work, Mom," Addy said. "I'll do more homework during free periods. And on the bus." Addy paused before asking the awkward question. "Can we afford it?"

Addy's mom sighed. She closed her textbook. "Well, things are tight. But your birthday is coming up at the end of the month. You could ask your grandparents for the money. It could be

your gift. If that's what you really want."

Addy's mom looked at her curiously. "Why *are* you so interested all of a sudden? You never talked about the swim team before. I thought you'd given up on sports."

Addy shifted in her chair. She didn't know how to explain it to her mom. So she lied. "I don't know," she said. "I was in the pool area today. The idea just came to me. I thought swimming might be fun. Good exercise and everything."

"Well, it certainly will give you exercise." Her mom picked up the form. "It says you can have a two-week trial period. Why don't we give it until then to decide for sure?"

"Thanks, Mom!" Addy jumped up. She went to her room to pack a swim bag. She wouldn't need two weeks to decide. Tomorrow would be the beginning of a whole new Addy.

Chapter Five
The Test

Addy took Ana into the locker room again the next day. She put on her suit in the stall next to Ana's. She had grown a lot since August. The suit was a little tight. And a bit worn. She'd have to make do for today.

When Ana saw her in her suit, she giggled. Addy didn't know why, exactly. She did a quick mirror check. Everything was covered. But the suit made her look even taller than she normally did. Maybe it was because you could see so much of

her legs.

Addy wrapped a towel around her waist. She stuffed her thick, curly red hair under a swim cap. Then she grabbed Ana's hand and walked her to the pool.

Ana wasn't as scared today. She sat right down on the edge of the pool. But it looked like she planned to stay there.

Javi, on the other hand, was clearly in love with the water. He was already in the pool. He was having a splashing fight with Miguel. Addy hoped Ana was watching the fun. Maybe she would want to join in. But Ana shrank back every time the splashes came near her.

Addy sighed. She couldn't worry about that right now. She had to take her swim test.

She walked over to the team. Coach Meg said, "Hey, everybody! This is Addy. She's joining our team. Make her feel welcome." A few people

said "Hi" and "Hey, Addy."

"I've got to give Addy the swim test. Erin, run practice for a few minutes." Coach Meg turned to Addy. "Erin's our team captain," she said.

The girl with the freckles stepped forward. She called, "OK, team! Warm-ups!" There were a few groans as the swimmers got in the water. Erin stood on the side of the pool next to Coach Meg and called out instructions.

"Now, Addy," said the coach. "Tell me about your swimming history. Yesterday, you said you were an experienced swimmer. Where have you competed?"

"Oh, no," said Addy. "I haven't *competed*. I just meant that I've spent my whole life swimming. You, know, like at my grandparents' lake house and stuff." She saw Coach Meg raise an eyebrow. Addy quickly added, "I took lessons, too. Here. At The Club. Years ago. I know all the strokes."

"I see," said Coach Meg slowly. "Well, let's see what you can do. I want to look at your freestyle. Do a short swim. Just 100 meters."

"Sure!" said Addy. "Um, that means…?"

"There and back again," said Coach Meg. "Twice."

"Okay." Addy paused. "Should I get on the diving thingy?" She thought she heard a snort coming from Erin's direction.

"The block?" Coach Meg laughed. "No, just start from the deck." She saw the confusion on Addy's face. "The side of the pool. Where you walk. You *can* dive, can't you?"

"Oh, yeah," said Addy. "Really well." She wanted to impress the coach. "And I'll pick up on all this swim lingo in no time. You'll see." She saw Erin roll her eyes.

Coach Meg smiled. "It's no problem. It's new to everyone when they're a beginner."

"Well, I'm not exactly a beginner," said Addy.

She dropped her towel and walked to the side of the pool.

I'll show her how good I am, Addy thought.

Coach Meg pressed her stopwatch and said, "Go!" Addy dove into the water. She swam as fast as she could toward the other end. Coach Meg would see that she was a great swimmer.

She completed the first length. As she touched the wall, she thought, *This is a really big pool.*

She turned and started back. Her muscles were beginning to burn. But she kept pushing. She needed a good time. She touched the other wall.

Halfway. She started the third length. She thought, *This is supposed to be a short swim?*

Her strokes were getting weaker. It felt like the water was getting thicker. She touched the wall a third time.

She struggled back to the finish. *Can twelve-year-olds have heart attacks?* she thought. *Is this what it feels like to die?*

Finally, she reached the end. She clung to the edge of the pool, fighting for breath.

"Okay, Addy!" Coach Meg said. "Good! You were working hard."

Addy couldn't speak. She could see that Erin was trying not to laugh. Addy didn't want to throw

up in front her.

"You did 100 meters in two minutes and ten seconds," Coach said, glancing at her stopwatch.

Addy gasped, "Is that good? Good enough to compete?"

"Well…" Coach Meg said, "It's good for a beginner. Everyone starts somewhere. The time will come down. We'll teach you how to swim."

Addy wanted to ask about competing again. But the coach squinted down at her. Then moved closer. "And Addy," she said softly. "There's a hole opening up on the side of your suit. I'll get your towel."

Coach Meg clapped Addy's shoulder. "Great, Addy!" she said. She spoke louder than she needed to. "Really great! That's all I need for now. We'll get you in a practice group tomorrow." She handed Addy her towel.

Addy got out. She quickly wrapped the

towel around herself. She smiled weakly at Coach Meg. It was kind of the coach to cover for her. But Addy felt crushed. *We'll teach you how to swim? What have I been doing?*

Addy walked past Miguel's class. He was standing in the pool with Javi. They were both talking to Ana in Spanish. They were trying to get her to come into the pool. Ana was shaking her head. She wasn't going to move.

Not a great day for either of us, thought Addy. She went sadly back into the locker room.

Chapter Six
Highs and Lows

Addy showed up at swim team the next day wearing a new bathing suit. She felt hopeful. Sure, she thought, she needed to get in shape. Sure, she needed to learn terms and rules about swim team. And tweak a few things with her strokes. But that shouldn't take too long. She had four whole weeks to get ready for the next competition.

She stood a little apart from the group of kids standing on the deck. (*Deck! See? I'm already*

learning! Addy thought.) A few kids smiled at her. Erin said, "Hi." But they all kept chatting about their "splits." Addy guessed that word did not mean what she thought it did. She didn't join the conversation.

Meg came out of the coaches' office. She called out names of different swim groups. "Pikes! Lanes three and four. Sharks! Lanes one and two."

Coach Meg took a few minutes to get the Pikes going. So Addy watched Erin lead the Sharks into the water. They were clearly the best group of swimmers. When they dove in, they barely made a splash. They swam easily up and down the length of the pool. Many, many times. When they stopped, Erin barely looked out of breath.

"OK, Addy," Coach Meg said. "You're going to be with the Starfish. That's the training team."

Starfish? Addy thought. *That doesn't sound like a racing name.*

She glanced around at the kids who were left. They were all younger. And shorter. Much shorter. They looked up at her curiously. Addy felt like an object in a preschool game. The one that didn't belong with the others.

"So, 'training team.' What exactly does that mean?" she asked Coach Meg. She tried to sound casual.

"It means you are not quite ready to compete. Starfish work on perfecting their strokes, turns, and starts. And they swim lots of laps to gain endurance."

"Oh," Addy said. She tried to hide her

disappointment. "Cool. And how long does it usually take? To move up to the real team?"

"Training is part of the real team, Addy," Coach Meg said.

Addy nodded. She should have known a coach would say that.

"I mean, how long until I will be ready to compete?"

The coach shrugged. "It's different for everyone. Don't worry about that. Let's just set some goals for the next few days. You don't become a great swimmer overnight."

Coach Meg started running drills. The Starfish practiced diving off the block. They practiced flip turns. And they swam endlessly up and down their lanes. Coach would stop kids every once in a while. She'd correct the position of a hand or head. Or she'd fix a kick. She stopped Addy a lot. It seemed like Addy had been

swimming the wrong way her whole life. Coach Meg cared what every single muscle in her body was doing. At every single moment. It made Addy feel very clumsy. Like her swimming was getting worse, not better.

Addy was wiped out by the end of practice. But all she got from Coach Meg was, "Nice work, Addy."

Addy made her way back to the locker room. Swim lessons had started. Ana must have figured out the locker room by herself. She was in her suit. But she was sitting on the side of the pool. Again. She had her chin in her hands. Addy sat down next to her. "*Cómo estás*, Ana? How are you?"

Ana didn't speak. She sighed. Addy said, "Yeah, I had a rough practice, too."

Addy watched Miguel's class for a minute. Everyone but Ana was in the water. Javi was learning fast. He was already doing a back float.

Miguel caught Addy's eye. He nodded at her as if to say, "See what you can do."

Addy glanced back down at Ana. Then she saw the wading pool. She grabbed Ana's hand and said, "Come on."

Addy sat down in the wading pool. Cautiously, Ana sat down next to her. Addy started teaching her a silly hand-clapping song. Ana loved it. She picked up music so quickly. Soon, she was giggling and copying everything Addy did.

Addy reached the end of the song. She slapped the water on the last line. Ana was too caught up in the game to notice. She hit the water, too. It splashed up in her face. She froze. For a moment, Addy was worried that Ana would be upset. But Ana laughed.

They played the game again. And again. The splashes got bigger and bigger. By the end of the lesson, Ana was completely soaked.

As Addy walked Ana toward the locker room, Miguel winked at her.

"Nice work, Addy," he said.

And this time, she felt like she deserved it.

Chapter Seven
Treading Water

After that, Addy met Ana every day after swim team. Addy took her to the wading pool. Ana was getting more and more comfortable there. But she still wouldn't try the big pool.

The following Wednesday, Addy and Zoe were in the art room. They were hanging out with Noah. Noah practically lived in the art room. So if you wanted to see him, you went there. It was his home turf. Like the music room was for Addy. Or

the basketball court was for Zoe.

Zoe was working on homework. Addy was helping the art teacher, Hannah. She was organizing art supplies for the preschool class. Addy liked lining up the crayons, scissors, and glue sticks in bright-colored rows. It had been another hard swim practice. But organizing always helped Addy's mood. It made her feel like everything was right with the world.

Miguel stuck his head in the door. "Hey, Addy. Thanks for your work with Ana. I can't give her the time she needs. I've got too many other kids in the class. But she trusts you. You're doing great with her."

Addy shrugged. "I don't know about that. It's been a week. She still won't get in the big pool."

Miguel smiled. "You're measuring with the wrong ruler. Ana is scared of the water. You got

her to play in it. That's a huge step." He walked away.

Addy sighed. "Well," she said. "If Miguel thinks that's a win, I'll take it. I haven't had a lot of success lately."

Noah said, "Swim team?"

Addy nodded. She wasn't getting much better. She'd been going to practice every day. But Coach Meg kept correcting her position, her stroke, and her kick. Anything and everything.

At least it gave Addy time to catch her breath. Her 100-meter time had hardly changed.

There was one bright spot. She hadn't broken anything or anyone for over a week. Including herself. She was trying to be extra careful. The biology lab story was starting to die down.

But Coach Meg hadn't said a word about moving her up. She was still on the training team.

And it was hard to wait. The whole reason she was on the team was so she could compete. It was the only way to change the way people thought of her.

Meanwhile, Addy had seen Coach Meg talking to Miguel several times. She'd overheard Meg say to Miguel that Javi was "a natural." Addy thought Coach Meg was eyeing him for the team.

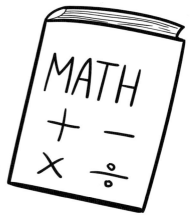

Addy's thoughts were interrupted by a groan from Zoe. "This stupid problem!" she said, pushing away her math book. "I've started over three times!" Zoe checked the time. "And I've got to get to basketball early. Our manager quit. I'm setting up for practice."

"Show me, Zoe," Addy said. She scanned the page. "Oh, I know what's wrong. Let me show

you…" And for the next ten minutes, she forgot her own problems. She was helping Zoe solve hers.

Addy's mom was asleep on the couch when Addy got home. A bunch of books lay around her. Addy looked at her mom for a minute. She thought her mom looked younger when she was asleep. Like the college freshman she'd been when Addy was born.

Her mom had worked hard. She'd finished school bit by bit. She got her college degree. She worked and took care of her baby. Addy's grandparents had helped where they could. But Mom had wanted to stand on her own two feet. Addy was proud of her.

Addy quietly put on the coffeepot and made some eggs. Then she woke her mom up. "Hey, Mom," she said. She handed her a steaming mug.

"You've got class soon."

"Thanks, honey," her mom said sleepily. She smelled the air. "You made dinner! You're such a sweetheart!"

They sat down together at the table. Addy looked at her mom's tired face. "How is class going?"

Her mom sighed. "Not great. The last couple assignments have been tough. The class I'm taking right now is really hard. A lot of students have dropped it. They're afraid they're going to fail."

"Why don't you drop it?" asked Addy.

"Aren't *you* afraid to fail?"

"Sure," her mom said. "But I love the subject. The class is hard. The hardest I've ever taken. But I enjoy the challenge." She ruffled Addy's hair. "And I have a good reason to be there. So I'll risk it." Her mom added, "How about you? How is swim going? Are you enjoying it?"

"It's OK," Addy said. "But I can't compete yet. The coach says I'm not ready."

"Is the competition so important?"

"Well, it's kind of the point, isn't it?" said Addy. "I mean, it's the reason to be on the team."

"But do you like the swimming part? Do you think you're becoming a better swimmer?" her mom asked.

Addy shrugged. "I guess."

Addy's mom didn't say any more.

She just sipped her coffee.

Chapter Eight
Blood in the Water

Addy pushed hard at swim team the next day. The next meet was getting closer. She needed to get better quickly.

When Addy finished the 100-meter freestyle drill, Coach Meg smiled. "Great job, Addy! You've knocked ten seconds off your time! Your hard work is paying off!"

"Am I fast enough to move up?"

"You're getting there. Your freestyle is definitely getting there. But we need to work on

your other strokes, too."

Addy tried to swallow her frustration. At this rate, the year would be over before she started competing. What would be the point then?

Coach Meg blew her whistle. "OK, team! Backstroke!"

Addy wanted to show the coach that her backstroke was in good shape. She made her way down the lane. She tried to get every detail of her form right. She made a perfect turn. She felt good. *Stay focused*, Addy thought. She hoped Coach Meg was watching.

Addy did stay focused on her form. But she forgot something else. She lost track of where she was in her lane. She drifted to one side. Her arm crossed the lane line. Smack! Her hand

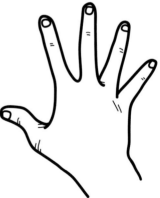

hit someone's face. It was Erin's.

Addy pulled up right away. "I'm so sorry!"

she said. But Erin was in no mood to hear her. Addy had hit Erin's nose. Hard. Blood was pouring down her face. "You're such a klutz!" Erin said angrily. "No wonder they call you Hurricane!" Her voice echoed around the room. She got out of the pool and grabbed her towel. She headed for the locker room to clean up.

There was an awkward silence. The whole team was looking at Addy. "She'll be okay," Coach Meg said kindly. "That kind of thing happens all the time. Just try not to drift in your lane." She got swim practice moving again. Then she went to check on Erin.

Addy felt guilty. And embarrassed. And

angry. After all, she'd made an honest mistake. It was an accident. Erin didn't need to yell at her in front of everybody.

Addy was still feeling hurt and humiliated at the end of practice. She walked over to meet Ana. Ana was waiting for her by the wading pool.

You and I need to get better faster, thought Addy. She took Ana's hand and led her back to the big pool. Ana sat down by the edge. She put her feet in the water. *Good. That's progress*, Addy thought. She sat down next to Ana. Addy started to kick. Ana copied her. The splashes got bigger and bigger.

Addy got in the pool. She let Ana splash water all over her. Ana laughed. Addy splashed water back at her. Ana screamed and laughed harder. *See?* Addy thought. *You're ready. It's time to move up*.

Addy scooped Ana up and pulled her into the pool. Addy held her tightly. She was careful to

keep Ana's head well above water. But she hadn't expected Ana to panic. Ana started screaming again. But this time, it was from fear.

Ana struggled in Addy's arms. She was trying to get out of the pool. Addy's grip slipped. Ana broke free. Her head went under.

Addy pulled Ana out as fast as she could. She sat her back on the edge. Ana was choking and shaking and sobbing. She was staring at Addy with wide, scared eyes.

"It's okay! It's okay," Addy said, trying to calm her down. "You're all right."

Now Miguel and Javi were there. Miguel was speaking to Ana in Spanish. Javi climbed out of the pool. He put his arm around his sister. Ana buried her head in his shoulder.

Miguel said, "Why don't you get her towel, Javi? Sit over on that bench. Help her calm down. She'll be okay in a minute."

Javi walked his sister over to the bench.

Miguel turned to Addy. "What happened? Everything was going so well."

"I know it was," Addy said. "But I thought… I thought she was used to the water. That it was time for her to get in. So I picked her up. She slipped…" Addy looked away. Her eyes were stinging. "I guess I pushed her too hard."

Miguel said, "Yeah, I guess you did. You've got to understand that everyone has their own clock." He put a hand on her shoulder. "Even you, Addy."

Addy brushed a tear away. So, Coach Meg and Miguel had been talking about her. Well, Miguel had been her Club director since she was four. He didn't miss much.

Miguel said, "Why don't you take Ana into

the locker room to change."

Addy nodded. "I will. But first, tell me how to say something."

When Addy walked over, Ana was calmer. But she still looked upset. Addy crouched in front of her. She took her hand.

"Por favor perdóname," Addy said. "Please, please, forgive me."

Chapter Nine
Flip Turn

Addy didn't go to swim practice the next day. She wanted a break. She asked Miguel if Ana could skip as well. Addy took her to the music room.

Ana acted a bit different with Addy at first. Not angry. Just…shy. Addy felt terrible. *She trusts you*, Miguel had said. Addy wanted to earn that back.

Addy and Ana sat in a quiet corner. Ana had the guitar. Addy had her violin. Ana played the little tune her father had taught

her. Addy picked it out on the violin. Addy played a simple melody. Ana figured it out on the guitar. They spent nearly all of Club doing this. It felt so easy and natural. Like fish in the water.

Near the end of Club, Addy took Ana to the art room. Javi was there. Then she went to the snack area to get something to eat. It took Addy a moment to recognize a girl sitting alone. She looked so different without her swim cap. It was Erin. She was working on homework.

Addy wanted to turn around. To leave the room. But she stopped herself. She'd have to get this over with at some point.

She walked up to the table. "Hey, Erin," Addy said. "I'm…I'm sorry about your nose." It looked bruised and swollen. She must have hit Erin pretty hard. Addy pointed to the vending machines. "Can I buy you a candy bar?"

To Addy's surprise, Erin just looked embarrassed. "It's okay," she said. "I actually did the same thing to someone four years ago. When I first joined the team. Coach Meg reminded me. Only I *broke* their nose." She smiled shyly. "But you *can* buy me a candy bar. Swimmers are always hungry."

They got their food and sat back down. Erin said, "You didn't come to swim today."

"No," Addy said. "I thought I could use a break. Or, maybe, that everyone else could. I haven't been the best team member."

Erin laughed.

"It takes time. Swimming is hard. Most of us have practiced four or five days a week for years. We've gone to camps. Had extra training. Don't measure yourself against us. We've been swimming forever. You really are getting better."

Addy felt shame. She realized how silly she

had been. She'd thought she could swim at Erin's level easily.

Addy remembered how long it had taken her to play the violin well. She'd spent most of her first year learning "Twinkle, Twinkle, Little Star." It had been frustrating. But she'd kept at it. Because she loved music.

What if Erin had waltzed into violin lessons one day, Addy thought, *and expected to learn the violin in just a few weeks?* Addy would have thought she was crazy.

Addy had wanted the success without the work. Because all she wanted from swimming was a trophy.

It was like Miguel had said. She had been measuring with the wrong ruler.

"I don't know how you do it," Addy said, shaking her head. "All that practice. Day in and day out."

Erin shrugged. "Practice is a drag. But I've never wanted to quit. I love being in the water. I love getting a little better every day. It's what keeps me going."

Addy nodded. It was time for her to catch her bus. She got up to go.

"And Addy," Erin said, "I'm sorry about what I said. I was just angry." There was a pause. "But is it true? Did they cancel your entire biology class?"

Addy smiled. "Yeah, they did."

Then she laughed. "They really, really did."

On Monday, Addy quit swim team. "It's not the right fit for me," Addy said to Coach Meg. "I like to swim. But I don't *love* it, if you know what I mean."

Coach Meg said she did. Later, Addy joined

Ana for swim lessons. They stayed in the wading pool the whole time. Addy got her to lie down in the water. She just touched her face to it. *Maybe tomorrow*, Addy thought, *we'll try blowing bubbles*.

"You and me, Ana," Addy said to her. "We're going to *own* this wading pool."

Addy joined her friends in the snack area later. She told them she had quit swim team.

"I'm not surprised," said Noah. "You were whining about it all the time."

"Well, it was a probably a good experience for you anyway," said Zoe.

"What do you mean?" said Addy.

"I mean that you finally tried something

hard. Usually, things are so easy for you."

Addy stared at her.

"You know what I mean," Zoe said. "You're good at all sorts of things. Violin, organizing stuff, babysitting, school. School, especially. You never have trouble with math. Sometimes I'm so jealous."

Javi nodded. "Yes," he said. "Good teacher."

Addy didn't know what to say. There was silence for a moment.

Milo broke in on her thoughts. "Well, what are you going to do instead?" he asked. He was carefully writing a title on a blank page of his field guide. *Pinus Strobus – Eastern White Pine*.

"I don't know," Addy said. "I'd like to be on a team. But sports aren't my thing."

"They're not mine either," said Noah. "But I don't mind. I'm a loner artist type."

They all laughed.

Then Zoe slammed her palm down on the table. "Addy," she said. "I know! Be my new team  manager. For basketball. You'd be great at it!"

Addy raised her eyebrows. "You sure you want to risk it? You do remember who you're talking to, don't you?"

"Sure I do," said Zoe, smiling. "You're our own perfect storm. You're Hurricane Addy."

And somehow, when Zoe put it that way, Addy didn't mind so much.

Want to Keep Reading?

Turn the page for a sneak peek at
the next book in the series.

ISBN: 9781538382394

Chapter One
The Tornado

"**N**oah, draw me another space alien!" Isaiah said, running away from him. He was heading for Noah's art table. Noah caught his little brother. He sat him back down on the front hall stairs. "Not now, Isaiah," he said. "It's time for school. You've got to put on your rain boots." He tried to push a boot over a wiggling foot.

"School!" Isaiah said. "Who cares about school?" Noah agreed. School was not his favorite thing either. But he always went. Going to school

meant going to his after-school program at The Club. And going to The Club meant going to the art room. And the art room was Noah's favorite place in the world.

"Isaiah…would…you…sit…still!" Noah said as he forced the second boot on. They were definitely tight. There were seven kids in the house. They didn't get a lot of new stuff. They waited until an older kid grew out of something. Isaiah would have to wait until eight-year-old Xavier outgrew his boots. With one final push, Noah got the boot on. Isaiah laughed and ran into their cramped living room. He dove onto the couch. Noah sat back on his heels and looked around. There were people everywhere.

Xavier was sitting on a chair arm practicing his violin. Noah's twin sister, Zoe, was standing near the TV. She was braiding nine-year-old Taylor's hair and watching basketball playoff

highlights. At the same time, Taylor was telling the world about her latest third-grade drama. She didn't seem to mind if anyone was listening or not.

Noah's stepmom was calling to his older brother Damian from the kitchen. She wanted him to walk their oldest sister, Lauren, home from work after his wrestling practice. Their neighborhood could be a bit unsafe after dark. Lauren was in the kitchen, too. She was arguing that she didn't need a bodyguard. Noah's dad was putting lunches in the backpacks lined up near the door. He was telling everyone to hurry up. He needed to walk them to their bus stop and catch the train to work.

Noah squeezed his eyes shut. He did this when he was thinking about drawing. *If I tried to draw my family,* he thought, *I'd make it look like a tornado. A big tornado with me lost in the middle.*

Noah usually felt lost in the middle. He was nine minutes younger than Zoe. That made him

the middle child. His family was big, busy, and loud. It was hard to stand out in it. He wasn't the youngest, the oldest, the shortest, the tallest, the smartest, the sportiest, the most popular, or the most musical. He wasn't even the only kid who was thirteen. He had just one thing that made him special. He was good at art.

Dad blew his whistle. "All right, Spencer family, let's roll!" he said. He was a high school gym teacher. The tornado started to move with cries of, "Ow, Isaiah! Stop it!" "That's *my* umbrella!" and "Don't step on my violin case!" *Eight hours*, Noah thought. It was eight hours before he could be in the art room. His fingers wanted to draw already.

Noah stood up. He grabbed Isaiah's hood as he headed toward the art table again. "Wrong way, Isaiah," he said, turning him around. "We gotta go to school." Isaiah groaned.

Noah guided his brother toward the door. He looked down at his frowning face. "But listen. I'll draw you a space alien when we get on the bus," he said.

"With tentacles?" said Isaiah.

Noah smiled. "Tentacles are my specialty." They walked out the door together and into the early spring rain.

ABOUT
the
AUTHOR

Elizabeth Gordon has a master's degree in Children's Literature from Hollins University. She was a finalist for the Hunger Mountain Katherine Paterson Prize for Young Adult and Children's Writing, the winner of the Hollins University Houghton Mifflin Harcourt Scholarship, and winner of the SCBWI Barbara Karlin Grant. She has published nine middle grade books so far, including a five-book superhero series.

the CLUB

MILO ON WHEELS
Elizabeth Gordon

Javi Takes a BOW
Elizabeth Gordon

Addy's Big Splash
Elizabeth Gordon

NOAH the CON ARTIST
Elizabeth Gordon

Club ZOE
Elizabeth Gordon

Check out more books at:
www.west44books.com

An imprint of Enslow Publishing

WEST 44 BOOKS™